SARAI

AND THE AROUND THE WORLD FAIR

SARAI GONZALEZ
AND
MONICA BROWN

SCHOLASTIC INC.

Text copyright © 2019 Sarai Gonzalez
Illustrations by Christine Almeda © 2019 Scholastic Inc.

ISBN 978-1-338-26095-3

10 9 8 7 6 5 4 3 2 1   19 20 21 22 23

Printed in the U.S.A.   40

First printing 2019

Book design by Carolyn Bull

To my loving grandparents Mama Chila and
Papa Carlos, for always believing in me and
supporting my dreams. Thank you!!
-SG

For Jeff, once again and always.
-MB

CONTENTS

INTRODUCTION

☆ ♡ ☆

SATURN-DAY

Saturdays are my favorite days. I even like the sound of the word "Saturday." It makes me think of the planet Saturn, so far away, floating in space. Saturn has pretty rings around it. Saturn is a colorful planet, and Saturdays are colorful days! I like to be creative on Saturday, with my baking or dancing or with an art project or even just a meeting of the Super-Awesome-Sister-Cousin Fun Club!

Because Saturdays are for family too. My little sisters and I get to be together all day, which doesn't happen during the week because my sister Josie goes to a different school from Lucía and me. After being in school all week, it's fun to wake up and know that we can do anything we want. Well, maybe not *anything* we want. Mom and Dad would have something to say about that.

Saturdays are also yummy food days. We usually start with a special breakfast that Dad makes—one of our favorites, like pancakes or waffles. And bacon of course! I like the sizzle and the smell that lasts in the house all day long. This morning Dad made me a pancake shaped like Saturn! Then Josie asked for a star, and Lucía asked for Pluto.

"I think that would just be a circle," Dad said, smiling.

"But *I'll* know it's Pluto!" Lucía said, and we all laughed.

Today is Saturday, Saturn-day, my favorite day. I wonder what fun the day will bring!

CHAPTER 1

BYE-BYE, BIBI

"Let's ride our bikes!" Josie signs and says.

"Yeah!" says Lucía. "Let's bike to the park. I'll race you both!"

"I'd rather walk to the park," I say.

"Why, mi estrella?" Tata asks. "Mi estrella" means his shining star.

"I thought you loved riding bikes!" Mama Rosí says. My grandparents are watching us so my parents can go out on a date for their wedding anniversary.

"I do like biking," I say. "I just don't feel like it today. Let's walk to the park."

"Walking is too slow!" says Lucía. "Don't you want to ride fast, Sarai?" That sounds fun, but the problem is, my old bike is too small. My knees bend so much that they bump the handlebars.

"I can't ride fast on Bibi anymore," I confess. "I'm too tall." My bicycle is named Bibi. I got it when I was six and back then I thought bicycles should have names. Now Josie rides Bibi more often than I do because it's just the right size for her.

"You've grown a lot this year," Mama Rosí says, "like a tree reaching up to the sky. Maybe it's time for a new bike."

Lucía got a new bike for her birthday last year, and it's awesome. It's purple with pink and white plastic ribbons that fly in the wind when she rides it. I'm a little jealous. I know I can ask for a bicycle for my birthday next year, but my birthday is so far away and I also know bicycles are expensive. I don't really like asking my parents for expensive things because sometimes it's hard for the Gonzales family five. Mom goes to work, and Dad stays home with us, which, he reminds us, is *a lot of work too.*

He spends a lot of time in our family's minivan, which we call the rectangle, driving us to our activities. Plus, he drives my sister Josie to her school for deaf and hearing-impaired children, which is far away. Luckily, my Tata helps watch my sister Lucía and me after school. It seems like there are always bills to pay, and I don't want my parents to worry about buying me new things. I have a coffee can where I've been saving for my new bicycle, but the last time I checked it only had eight dollars.

"I don't want a new bike right now," I say, not quite telling the truth. "Though I do think it might be time to say bye-bye to Bibi and give her to Josie."

Josie points at the bike. "I can have Bibi?" she asks.

"Yes" is one of the words I know in sign language, so I turn to Josie and make a big show of giving Josie my bike. She jumps up and down and hugs me so hard I think I might break.

Josie hands me her scooter, climbs on Bibi, and takes off for the park.

I scoot slowly, and Mama Rosí walks next to me. Tata has to jog to keep up with Josie and Lucía. They know the rules, though, so they stop at each stop sign and wait for Tata to catch up. Then they cross the street together. When we're almost at the park, I kick my feet out and ride the scooter as fast as I can. But if I'm being honest, I'm a little jealous.

Once we get to the park, I forget about not having Bibi and spend my time swinging as high as I can. Then I jump off the swings, and for a second, it feels like I'm Super Sarai, a girl who can fly! I land in the wood chips, and Tata says, "Good job, Sarai!"

"Thanks," I say, and run over to where Tata and Mama Rosí are resting on a bench.

"Have some water," Mama Rosí says. "It's hot." I take a cool sip, and then I hear someone say, "Hi, Sarai." I turn around and see my best friend from school, Christina. She's with her mom, and she's walking her little dog, Wolf. Wolf is so cute! She's got fluffy black fur.

"Hi, Christina! Hi, Ms. McKay," I say, and run up to give Christina a hug. Christina doesn't really hug me back because she's still a little shy sometimes. But she smiles.

"How are you?" I ask them both.

"Good!" Ms. McKay says, and walks over to say hello to my grandparents. My sisters run over to pet Wolf. They've met her before.

"Wolf is a scary name for such a nice dog," Lucía says.

"That's what everyone says," Christina says. "But dogs and wolves are related! They are both part of the canid family of animals, along with foxes and coyotes, just to mention a few." I love how many crazy facts Christina knows. She wants to be a writer when she grows up, and she's always researching one thing or another.

"How old is Wolf?" Josie asks.

"She'll be three this year," Christina says. Then she frowns.

"What's wrong?" I ask her.

"Well, I'm worried about Wolf," Christina says. "We're going out of town next weekend, and she'll have to be put in a kennel where she won't know anybody."

"Poor Wolf," I say. I love dogs, but Mom and Dad always say we don't have the time or space for a pet.

"I wish we could watch her," I tell Christina.

"Can't we?" Lucía says.

I bend down to pet Wolf. "What do you think?" I ask her.

Woof! Woof! Woof!

I laugh. "I was just thinking the same thing."

CHAPTER 2

THE FROG CAFÉ

Later that night, when Mom and Dad get home, we surprise them with a cake that says "Happy Anniversary to the Best Parents in the World." It's hard to fit all the words on the cake, but I manage it. I have to look up how to spell "anniversary," though. After we've eaten, we say goodbye to Tata and Mama Rosí and send them home with some cake. Then Lucía turns on some music, and we dance for a while. Mom says the Gonzalez girls have energy that they need to get out. Finally

a slower song comes on, and I can't help it—I let out a big yawn. Mom looks at Dad.

"It's time," she says to Dad. "I'll put Josie and Lucía to bed, and you can tuck in Sarai."

"Sounds like a plan," Dad says. "Sarai, go get ready for bed and let me know when you're ready."

Some people might say that ten is too old to be tucked in by your parents, but I don't care. When else can I have my dad or mom all to myself? Besides, I can usually talk Dad into telling me a story about when he was little in Costa Rica. After I get ready for bed, I get under the covers and say, "I'm ready! Come say good night."

My dad comes in, sits on the edge of my bed, and gives me a kiss on the forehead.

"Tell me a story from when you were a kid!" I ask Dad.

"But it's late," Dad says. "You need to sleep, Sarai."

"A quick one! Pretty please with sugar and three cherries on top?" I ask. "How about when you used to go and help your uncles pick coffee beans in the fields? Or when you and your cousins used to hunt possums and armadillos in the rain forest? Or maybe you can talk about your grandfather's bakery?"

"See," Dad says, laughing, "you've heard every story already! I don't have any left."

"I bet you can think of something," I tell him. "You are my dad full of stories!"

"Hmmmmmmm," he says, like he's thinking hard. "I know. Have I ever told you the story of Café la Rana?"

"No, you haven't!" I say excitedly. "I would definitely remember if you told me a story about a frog café."

"Okay," Dad says, "well, once, when I was a little boy in Costa Rica, we were on a weekend trip to the ocean. On the way, we stopped in a little town we had never been to before. In the middle of the town was a little café called Café la Rana. We sat down to order our food, and my mother, your Mama Chila, said, 'I wonder why they call this the Frog Café?'"

"Why did they?" I interrupt.

"Shhh," Dad says, "listen to the story and you'll find out."

"Okay," I say, and pretend to zip my lips.

"We order our food and are waiting for it, when all of a sudden we hear a noise," Dad says. "It sounded like this: croá . . . croá . . . croá." I start laughing at my silly dad, croaking like a frog.

"Dad! You're so silly! I thought frogs say ribbit!"

"This was a Costa Rican frog, and trust me, they say croá," Dad says. "Your poor grandmother. Mama Chila was just about to take a sip of her café, and splash! The frog landed right inside her cup. She yelled and dropped the cup onto the table, and it spilled everywhere! Later, we saw frogs in the bathroom, the parking lot, *everywhere*!"

"Well, now I know why it was called Café la Rana!" I say, laughing. "Poor Mama Chila."

"She was fine, and we never forgot the Frog Café."

Then I get an idea. "Dad, can I have a pet frog? They're so cute!"

"No way!" Dad says, shaking his head. "Absolutely not."

"But wouldn't it be great to have a pet?" I ask.

"We don't have the time or space for a pet," Dad says, for the hundredth time.

"Do we have time to watch someone else's pet, like for a weekend?" I ask.

"I'm confused," Dad says. "Who wants us to watch their pet?"

"Christina," I say. "She's going out of town next weekend and needs someone to watch her dog. Wolfie is little, so she doesn't take up much space. Besides, we have a fenced yard. I thought it could be fun."

"That's a big responsibility, Sarai," Dad says, "even if it is only for a weekend."

"But responsibility is my middle name!" I say. "Don't I help with the girls, and do my chores, and—"

"Let me talk to your mom," Dad says, cutting me off.

"Yay!" I say.

"I didn't say yes, yet," Dad says, standing up. "Good night, Sarai. Sweet dreams."

"Croá! Croá!" I croak back. "That's how frogs say good night."

CHAPTER 3

ALL AROUND THE WORLD

When I walk into class Monday morning, I notice a big globe sitting on Ms. Moro's desk. It's twice the size of a basketball.

"What's that for?" I ask her.

"You'll see!" she says, smiling. Ms. Moro smiles a lot, and I like that. She always seems happy to see us. After the bell rings, Ms. Moro takes roll, and then she stands up and gives the globe a spin. The different colors of the countries and the blue ocean blur together.

"I have a special announcement," Ms. Moro says. "Martin Luther King Jr. Elementary is going to have an Around the World fair!"

"What's that?" asks Ellie.

"It's an opportunity for everyone to learn about different countries," she says. "Each of you will select a country, and then you will work on a trifold poster with facts and pictures related to the nation of your choice. You will also bring in some snacks from the nation you are representing to share with others. We'll set up our poster boards in the school gym and invite everyone to go exploring around the world."

"I choose Jamaica!" Ellie says. "That's where my family is from, and I go back every summer."

"I'll sign you up for Jamaica, Ellie," Ms. Moro says. "You can choose a country that represents your family heritage or one that isn't related to you at all. Perhaps some of you will want to choose a country you know absolutely nothing about. Others may wish to learn more about your ancestors' country or share your home culture with others. The important thing is that we all learn from one another."

First I think I want to choose Peru, the country where my mother was born. But then I think that I'd like to choose Costa Rica, the place my father and his parents, my Mama Chila and Papá, are from. I want everyone to know about my family history.

"What if we can't decide which country to choose?" I ask.

"Then I'm happy to assign you one. We want to learn about as many countries as possible. Related to the Around the World fair," Ms. Moro continues, "I'd like to share a few facts with you. We have nine different language groups represented at this school and families with heritage in over seventeen countries!

ooh!

"Because we are such a diverse school, we've decided to create an Around the World cookbook, from our students. Each of you can contribute one favorite family recipe."

"I have so many great family recipes!" I say. "Ceviche, arroz con pollo, olla de carne—"

"She said *one*," Valéria says, cutting me off.

"Let's not interrupt each other," Ms. Moro reminds us gently.

"Can I sign up for Mexico?" Auggie asks.

"Yes," says Ms. Moro. "I'll pass around a sign-up sheet right now and then put it up on the bulletin board. You need to pick a country by the end of the week. Let's brainstorm. What kind of things do you want to learn about your country?"

"Language?" I say.

"Yes!" says Ms. Moro. "What else?"

"What the flag looks like?" Christina asks.

"The types of food they eat!" Kayla suggests.

"The history of the country," Auggie says.

"These are all great suggestions!" says Ms. Moro, passing out handouts. "You can also explore things like the politics, art, literature, and music of your country. Here's the assignment information."

I have so many thoughts going through my head. Should I choose Peru? Costa Rica? Or somewhere completely different?

"Guess what?" I announce at dinner that night. "Our school is going to have an Around the World fair."

"The first graders are doing it too!" Lucía says. "We'll be learning and singing songs from Kenya, Morocco, and South Africa!"

"I want my school to have an Around the World fair," Josie signs and says.

"Maybe we can suggest it to your teachers, Josie," Dad responds.

"Great idea!" Mom says. "Are you excited, Sarai?"

"I am," I say. "Except I have a problem. I need to choose a country, and I can't decide between Costa Rica and Peru. I want to represent my culture at the fair, but I'm not one or the other—I'm both!"

"You are both," Dad says, "and a citizen of the United States."

"We are all citizens of the world," Mom says, smiling. "Of course you want to celebrate all the parts of you."

"I'm going to ask if I can choose two countries," I decide. "Ms. Moro is the nicest teacher ever. She'll help me figure it out."

"So," says Lucía, "did Sarai tell you that we saw Christina and her mom and her really well-behaved dog Wolf at the park on Saturday?"

I try to hide my smile. I know where my littlest sister is going with this.

"She did," Dad says.

"And? Can we babysit Wolf this weekend?" she asks.

"Taking care of a dog is a lot of work," Mom says, "even if it is only for two days. When I was a little girl, we had a pet dog named Ruthie, and one day when we weren't paying attention, we left the gate open and Ruthie went missing. I thought I lost Ruthie forever, and it was the worst day of my life. I was so sad I cried myself to sleep that night."

"Oh no!" Josie signs and says. "What happened to Ruthie?"

"Did she ever come back?" Lucía asks.

"My uncle found her the next afternoon. She had followed a neighbor home from school. Luckily, my uncle overheard the boy's father talking about the dog at the butcher. But after that, we were always careful to latch the gate. I think if we are going to let you watch Wolf, you need to show us just how responsible you can be."

"Yes, I agree," Dad says, looking at Mom. I think I see him wink. What's going on here? "Responsible girls clean their own rooms and organize their toys and help around the house without being asked."

"If we clean up our rooms and do extra chores, can we watch Wolf?" Lucía asks, excitedly. I've never seen her excited to clean anything before.

"That sounds fair to me," Mom says. "You know, watching Wolf will be a lot of work. It's not as easy as it seems. You have to walk a dog and make sure they have water and food. You also have to take them out to go to the bathroom several times a day, and keep them out of trouble."

"And clean up after them," Dad says.

"Yes!" I say. "We can do it. Now can we be excused? We've got some cleaning to do!"

THE BIG DECISION

"Hi, Ms. Milligan!" I say to my favorite librarian ever. It's library day, so our class gets to spend time in the library after lunch. "What's been going on, girls?" asks Ms. Milligan. I can tell she's the kind of teacher who cares about our lives.

"We're having an Around the World fair!" says Christina, louder than usual. Even Christina feels comfortable with Ms. Milligan.

Ms. Milligan laughs. "How fun," she says in a library whisper. "What country did you girls choose?"

"I chose Ireland," Christina says.

"I love Ireland!" Ms. Milligan says. "I backpacked around Ireland after I graduated from library school. It's such a wonderful country."

"I'm still deciding between *two* wonderful countries and that's my problem," I tell Ms. Milligan. "I don't know if I want to choose Peru, where my mom was born, or Costa Rica, where my dad was born."

"Well, they're both amazing places, so I can see why it's a tough choice," Ms. Milligan says.

"Why don't you do some research so you can make a more informed decision?"

"That's exactly what I'm going to do!" I say, and then I start looking for books on Costa Rica and Peru. By the time I'm done, I have a stack that's almost too big to carry. I take it to one of the library tables and get out my notebook. I make two columns. One says "Peru" and the other says "Costa Rica." I start taking notes on interesting facts.

Peru

-Continent of South America
-Official languages: Spanish, Quechua, Aymara
-Home of the Inca Empire
-Capital is Lima
-Shaped like a foot!
-Where potatoes are from!
-Home to llamas and alpacas (they are so cute!!)

Costa Rica

- Located in Central America, on the continent of North America
- Official language: Spanish

¡hola!

- Located on an isthmus (look up definition of isthmus!) between the Pacific Ocean on the west and the Caribbean Sea on the east
- Name means "rich coast"
- Capital is San José
- The singer Chavela Vargas is from Costa Rica!
- September 15, 1821: Independence Day from Spain
- Home to howler monkeys and TWO kinds of sloths!

Before I know it, library period is over. I've barely even started taking notes! And both Costa Rica and Peru are so interesting I'm no closer to deciding which country to pick. I check out a couple books on each, and then head back to Ms. Moro's room with the rest of my class.

"Did you get some good research done?" I ask Christina as we walk back.

"Yes!" Christina says. "I've been reading about leprechauns! There are so many mythical creatures in Ireland."

"What are leprechauns like?" I ask Christina, smiling. I know how much she loves fantasy things.

"They are like fairies," she says. "They're little and they mend shoes and they like to play jokes. If you catch one, they will grant you three wishes!"

"I think it would be mean to try to catch a fairy," I say.

"I agree," says Christina. Then she tells me about a prehistoric monument in England called Stonehenge. It sounds amazing.

"Maybe we can visit Ireland together some day!" I say. "Maybe we can go to Costa Rica, and Peru, too."

"Why stop there?" Christina says. "We can take an Around the World tour!"

"Yes!" I say. "Maybe when we are really old, like twenty."

"Yeah," says Christina. "Let's do it."

We will. I just know it.

CHAPTER 5

THE NEW OLD BIKE

When Lucía and I get home from school, Tata is waiting on the porch as usual.

"Hi, Tata! Can I have a snack?" Lucía asks. "I'm extra hungry!"

"Me too," I say. Cafeteria food is never as good as my Mama Rosí's.

"Of course," Tata says. "But first, come into the garage! I have a something to show you." Tata seems really excited and happy. He was an electrician before he retired, so I figure he has some new

gadget to work on—a radio or a typewriter or an old machine of some kind. The only thing Tata likes better than tinkering is going to garage and yard sales to find things to tinker with. "This surprise is especially for you, Sarai," he says.

"Really?" I say. Now I'm curious. What kind of surprise is just for me? We walk over to the garage, and there is something lumpy under a tarp.

"What is it, Tata?" Lucía asks. "Can it be a surprise for me too?"

"Eventually," Tata tells Lucía. "But right now, this surprise is for your sister. Ready for the unveiling?"

"Yes!" I say, jumping up and down. With a dramatic whoosh, Tata lifts off the tarp, and that's when I see it. It's a *really* old bicycle with a broken

brake pad and no ribbons on the handlebars. It's a couple of different colors but mostly brown and silver where the metal shows through the paint. The front tire is missing, and the back wheel has a bunch of broken spokes.

"Eww," says Lucía. "I mean, wow."

"Is that for me?" I ask Tata in a small voice.

"Yes!" he says. "I bought it for cheap at a garage sale, and I thought I could fix it up for you! Is it the right size?" Tata seems really excited, and I don't want to disappoint him, so I stand up next to the bike and hold on to the handlebars. The seat is cracked and doesn't look comfortable, but I sit on it anyway.

"It is," I say. "But where's the chain?"

"I have to get a new one. The important thing is that the body is solid and the size is just right! We'll have you biking everywhere before too long!" Tata says. "It needs to be sanded, and we need to get some paint, replace the brake pads—"

"But that's so much work!" I say. "I can just save up for a new bike."

"This will be better than any bike you could find in a store by the time we are done with it, Sarai," Tata says. "You've just got to have vision! When I was a young boy in Peru, I would fix things too. My father taught me, and now I can teach you."

"Thanks so much, Tata," I say. I don't want the old broken-down bike I see in front of me, but I don't want to hurt Tata's feelings either. "I bet it will turn out great."

"Someday, you'll inherit the bike, Lucía," Tata says. She doesn't look too excited about that possibility.

I stare at Lucía until she says, "Cool."

"Now who wants a snack?" Tata asks. "Mama Rosí sent over some arroz con pollo."

"I do!" Lucía says, but all of a sudden I'm not feeling very hungry.

CHAPTER 6

HALF OF SOMETHING

It seems like every day after school, Tata wants to work on my bicycle. I want to paint it, but Tata says we need to sand the surface first. It takes forever! I'm glad we get to watch Wolf this weekend because I need something to look forward to.

I think that Tata realizes I'm not having too much fun, because on the second afternoon of bike fixing, he says, "Sarai, algo es algo. Menos es nada."

"Something is something? Less is nothing?

I don't get it," I tell Tata. Sometimes I don't understand all the Spanish phrases he uses.

"It means half of something is better than nothing at all," he says. I look down at my bike with the missing wheel, and I can't help it. I finally let out my feelings.

"How do you know? I'd rather have nothing at all than half a bike!" Then I run into the house and into my room. I slam the door and lie down on my bed. I don't want to sand an old bike. I want a new bike. I end up falling asleep, and when I wake up, my parents are home and my Tata has left. Now I feel sort of bad. I know Tata was just trying to do a nice thing for me. And really, he's pretty much always doing nice things for me.

⋄✶ ♡✶⋄

The next day, when Lucía and I come home from school, I see Tata is in the garage, hard at work on the bike. He sees me, smiles, and stands up. I walk over and give him a hug.

"It's done!" Tata says. "No more sanding. We can choose a paint color now."

"I'm so sorry," I tell Tata, squeezing him tight. "Lo siento." Tata loves it when I speak Spanish.

"It will be okay," Tata says. "Don't worry, mi estrella." I'm glad I'm still Tata's star.

"It's looking good!" Lucía says, like she's surprised. Tata laughs and says, "I told you, we just need to envision how great this bike will be. That and hard work usually do the trick."

"Vision," I say. "I don't have it, but I'm gonna get it!"

"That's the spirit!" Tata laughs, and I do too. I love pink and purple, but when we look at paint colors, I decide to be a little different and choose a pretty orange color. Tata likes it too.

When I get to school the next morning, all anyone can talk about is the Around the World fair and the Around the World cookbook.

"I'm bringing pan dulce to the fair!" says Auggie.

"What's that?" asks Christina.

"It's Mexican sweetbread. We have it on weekends and dip it in our café con leche," Auggie says.

"Your parents let you have coffee?" I ask Auggie.

"A little," he says. "It's mostly hot milk."

"I love coffee," I say, "but Mom says that's the last thing I need. I guess I have a lot of energy to begin with."

"You do," Christina agrees, and I laugh.

"Ellie, what are you making for the fair?"

"I want everyone to try my mom's coconut rice and red beans," Ellie says. "Though it was hard

to choose just one recipe for the cookbook—there are so many yummy Jamaican foods. And I'm also going to share Jamaican music. Did you know that reggae and ska music were created in Jamaica?"

"I didn't!" I tell Ellie. "I can't wait to hear it."

"Speaking of our Around the World fair, today is the final day to sign up!" Ms. Moro says at the beginning of class. "I'll pass around the sign-up sheet so you can see who has been assigned what so far. I'd like to see as many countries represented as possible, so don't sign up for a country that someone else has already claimed."

When the list makes its way to my desk, I see lots of countries: Canada, Mexico, Guatemala, Vietnam, Jamaica, Columbia, China, Israel, Egypt, Kenya, Chile, Iran, Turkey, Cabo Verde. I'm surprised to see that Valéria has signed up for Peru.

"Since when are you interested in Peru?" I ask her. I happen to know that her family is Brazilian.

"Since always," Valéria says. "I want to visit someday. I have a cousin that lives there."

"That's actually really cool," I say, and smile at Valéria. She doesn't smile back, but that's okay because she made my choice easy. I write down Costa Rica. I can't wait for the fair!

CHAPTER 7

ADVENTURES WITH WOLF

Between working on my poster for the fair and working on my bike with Tata, it seems like the week flew by. Tata and I spray-paint my bicycle orange, and I have to admit, it's starting to look nice. Tata fixes the chain with my help, and somewhere he finds an almost-new bike seat that is silver and sparkly.

"Wow," I tell Tata on Friday after school. "My new bicycle is looking good!"

"Isn't it?" Tata says. "I need to find the perfect

front wheel. I just heard about a secondhand bicycle store that has a bunch of used parts."

"Great!" I say, running my hands over my bright orange bike. "Because I'm ready to ride!"

Tata, Lucía, and I drive over to the bike shop, which is called the Recycled Bicycle, and we have lots of fun. We even find a pole with a pretty flag to attach to the back of my bike! Everything is coming together, and soon, my bike should be ready to ride.

"It's Wolf weekend! It's Wolf weekend!" Lucía sings. It's evening, and we've cleared the table and done the dishes. The whole family is waiting for Christina and her mom to drop off Wolf on their way to the airport.

"When are they going to get here? I can't wait!" Josie signs and says.

"Me too!" I say. "Can Wolf sleep in my room?"

"I want Wolf to sleep in my room!" Lucía says.

"But Christina's my friend, not yours," I say.

"Well, I'm the one who talked Mom and Dad into letting us watch her in the first place," Lucía says, putting her hands on her hips. That's never a good sign.

"I know!" I say, "since it's a special weekend, can we all sleep out here in the family room with Wolf?"

"Yes!" Josie signs and says. "Let's have a slumber party!"

"It will be like a sleepover, but in our own house!" I say.

"We can make Wolfie an honorary member of the Super Awesome Sister Fun Club!" Lucía says.

Super★Awesome
♥Sister♥
FUN CLUB!
Reading Corner

"They're here!" Josie signs and says. Josie, Lucía, and I race to the door. I get there first, and open it.

"Hello!" I say. Christina is holding Wolf, and she doesn't look like she wants to let go of her, but Wolf is extra wiggly. Christina puts her down, and she comes straight to me.

"Thanks so much for helping us out," Ms. McKay tells my mom and dad.

"Of course," Mom says. "It's our pleasure."

"I've made a list to remind you of what do," says Christina. She's very serious. I can tell she's worried about leaving her dog. Ms. McKay gives Dad a bag that has Wolf's food and toys in it. "Make sure the gate in your backyard is shut before you let Wolf play out there. I don't want her to run away! And when you walk her, she needs to be on her leash at all times. Also, you really need to watch her because she likes to get into things and she still chews things she shouldn't sometimes." I nod at Christina.

"You can trust me," I say. "I'll watch her every second."

"Great," Christina says. "I know you'll give Wolf lots of love." We talk a little bit more and take Wolf into the backyard for a little bit, but pretty soon Ms. McKay says that they have to go or they'll miss their plane. They're visiting family in California for the weekend.

"See you on Sunday!" I say. We spend the rest of the evening playing with Wolf, who loves to play fetch and yips and yaps a lot.

"For a little dog, she sure makes lots of noise," Dad says.

"You guys are keeping Wolf too busy to get into any trouble," Mom says. "Great idea." I fall asleep with Wolf cuddled up next to me on the couch.

I wake up, as usual, with the sun. It's streaming into the family room and into my eyes. Lucía and Josie are sound asleep in their sleeping bags on the floor. It's quiet. Too quiet. I sit up straight.

"Where's Wolf?" I wonder aloud. "Wolf! Where are you?" Lucía and Josie grumble and start to wake up. I look all over the family room and the kitchen, and Wolf is nowhere to be found. I wake up my sisters. "Mom! Dad! Wolf is missing!"

"That's impossible," says Lucía sleepily. "Before we went to bed, Mom and Dad checked that all the doors in the house were shut."

"We've been in here all night!" I say. "How could Wolf get out?"

"Well, I haven't been in here all night," Josie signs and says. "I got cold, so I went in my room to get another blanket. But I came right back out."

"I wonder if Wolf followed you," I say. "Let's check your room."

We go into Lucía and Josie's room, tiptoeing so we don't wake up our parents. Sure enough, there's Wolf. Only Wolf doesn't look like Wolf. She looks like a purple monster. She's covered in tempera paint!

"Oh no!" Lucía says. "She got into our paints. How did one little dog make such a mess?" I run and get paper towels but I feel like I'm just spreading the paint around the girls' room.

"Ugh, it looks like she chewed through the paint bottle. Is she going to be okay?" I ask. "Christina is going to be so mad at me! We need to tell Mom and Dad."

"Sweetheart, tempera paint is nontoxic, thank goodness," Mom says as she walks into the room and looks at the damage. Dad is right behind her. "But it looks like Wolf got more paint on her than in her anyway."

"What a mess!" Josie signs and says, and I agree. There are purple paw prints everywhere.

"This dog needs a bath," Dad says, picking up Wolf. Wolf doesn't want to be picked up and wiggles free immediately and runs out of the room.

"Catch her!" Josie signs and says.

"She's getting paint everywhere!" I say as Mom, Dad, Josie, Lucía, and I chase Wolf around the house. She leaves a trail of paw prints.

"For a dog with such small little legs, she's fast!" Mom says.

"Well, I'm faster!" Dad says, finally catching Wolf and hugging her to his chest.

"Watch out!" I say. "You are getting paint on your pajamas!"

"Better that it gets on me than everywhere else in the house," Dad says, taking Wolf into the bathroom. "Don't worry, little one, you're just going to get a bath." I hear Dad starting the water and a few barks. I don't think Wolf likes being washed.

"I'm going to get the mop," Mom says. "Sarai, you get some towels and go help your father. Lucía, Josie, you help me clean up your room."

Wolf doesn't like being dried any more than she likes being washed. She shakes her whole body until Dad and I are both damp and smell like wet dogs.

"You were right," I tell Dad as Wolf wiggles out from under the towel. "Having a dog IS a lot of work."

When Christina picks Wolf up on Sunday night, the first thing she says when she sees Wolf is: "She looks so clean. Did you give Wolf a bath?" I confess what happened with the tempera paint, but luckily she isn't mad at all. Christina just says, "Wolf! You rascal!"

CHAPTER 8

COSTA·RICA
by Sarai Gonzalez

AROUND THE WORLD FAIR

The day of the Around the World fair is sunny and bright. I am so excited! Tata and Mama Rosí have promised to stop by my school to walk around the fairgrounds with me, which is really just our school gymnasium transformed by all our exhibits. Different classes take turns performing, and the gym is filled with the sounds of international music and people laughing and enjoying themselves. Outdoors there are games from around the world like Skippyroo Kangaroo

from Australia and Corre, corre la guaraca, a running game from Chile.

The fair is open-house style, and parents and family are invited to visit during the school day. I wish my parents were able to come, but Mom has to work and Dad will be picking Josie up at her school. I stand by my poster and share information about Costa Rica with everyone who stops by. I explain that my father was born there, and that he came to the United States as a little boy. I have

pan casero and bizcochos—homemade bread and biscuits like the kind my grandfather made in his bakery in Costa Rica.

"Sarai!" I hear my name called, and see Mama Rosí and Tata.

"Hi!" I say. "I'm so glad you could come!"

"I love your poster," Mama Rosí says.

"Thanks!" I say. "Isn't the Costa Rican flag cool?"

"It sure is," I hear another voice say. It's Mama Chila, my grandmother on my father's side!

"We picked up a surprise for you on the way to school," my Tata says, smiling, as Mama Chila wraps her arms around me. She lives kind of far away, so I'm sure Tata and Mama Rosí went way out of the way to get her and bring her to the fair.

"Mama Chila!" I say, hugging her. "I'm so happy to see you."

"There is no way I would miss my grand-daughter's presentation on Costa Rica. I've always thought our flag was beautiful. I like the way the Costa Rican coat of arms looks against the blue, white, and red bands."

"Are those mountains?" Mama Rosí asks, pointing to the flag.

"Those are three volcanoes representing the three mountain ranges in Costa Rica!" I tell Mama Rosí.

"And one star for each of the seven provinces of Costa Rica," Mama Chila says, patting my back. "One day we will visit them together."

"Your Papá would be here too if he didn't have a dentist's appointment today," Mama Chila says. "Now tell me what else you learned about my country!" I have so much to share. One of the things I'm most excited to talk about is the Monteverde Cloud Forest Preserve.

"Clouds always cover the trees like a blanket, and there is so much moisture, that plants thrive. Did you know there are over two thousand plant species in the cloud forest?" I ask my grandparents.

"We visited the preserve once," Mama Chila says, "when your father was about your age. It's truly beautiful."

After I share my poster with my grandparents, we go for a walk and visit all the other countries. We listen to Lucía's class perform their songs, and clap very loud. The festivities continue after school.

When we finally get home, Mom, Dad, and Josie are already there, and Mom suggests we all sit out on the porch and have a glass of chicha morada to cool off.

Tata says, "Sure, but I need to do something first." Then he disappears.

"Where's Tata going?" Lucía asks.

"Who knows?" Mama Rosí says. We are distracted from wondering by the tray of chicha morada Mom brings outside.

"This is delicious!" my Mama Chila says.

"Thanks! I made it myself with pineapple and spices and the purple corn Mr. Martínez sells at the store," Mom says. "It's Mama Rosí's recipe. Homemade is always best." Lucía, Mama Rosí, Mama Chila, and I are sitting and sipping and enjoying being together when all of a sudden we hear it.

"Woo-hoo!" Tata yells as he zooms out of the garage. He is riding my new bike! It has two wheels and everything! It looks amazing.

"WOW!" I say. "My bike looks awesome!"

"And it doesn't just look awesome," Tata says, driving in a circle. "It sounds awesome too!" Then he flicks a little silver bell on the handlebar.

Briiiiiiiiiing! Briiiiiiiiiiiing! My bike tinkles and rings!

"Tata, you rock!" Lucía says.

"Let's go for a bike ride!" Josie signs and says.

"Let's!" I say, jumping up and down.

"Are grandpas supposed to bike that fast?" Lucía asks, watching Tata do figure eights in front of our house.

"I don't know if they are supposed to, but this grandpa does!" says Tata. I run out to meet him.

"Want to give it a try?" Tata asks me, getting off the bike.

"Yes!" I say as Tata hands me my pink helmet. I climb on my new bike and give it a spin. It's the perfect height!

"Look at me go!" I say. I ride up and down our street with a big smile on my face. There are so many places I want to go, and right now, it feels like I can go anywhere and be anything. I pedal and the wind blows through my hair and, in my mind, I'm Super Sarai, flying fast on my bike, up, up, up and into the sky!

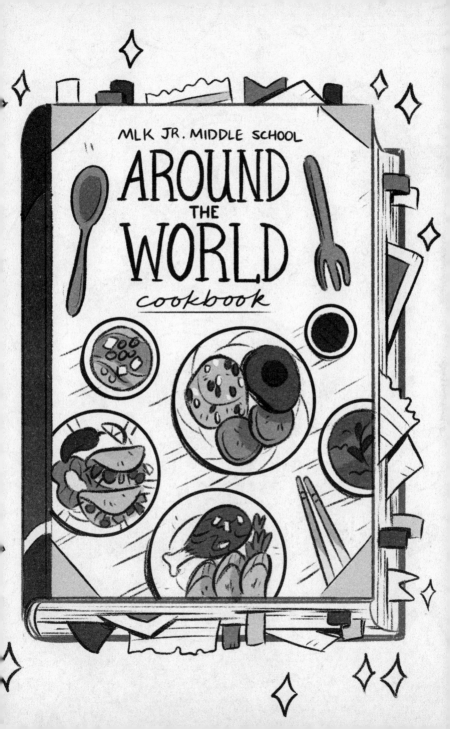

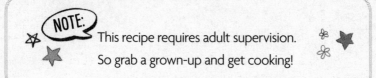

EMPANADAS

Empanadas are eaten all over Latin America, and they are prepared in different ways in each country.

MAMA ROSÍ'S PERUVIAN EMPANADAS

Serves 6

Note: The key ingredient to this recipe is ají panca paste. It is a kind of chili pepper that comes from Peru. You can buy it in most Spanish supermarkets.

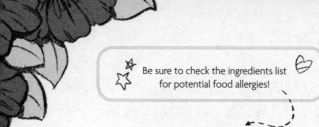

INGREDiENTS

1 lb. all-purpose flour

2 tsp. salt, divided

1 stick of butter (4 oz.)

⅓ cup vegetable oil, divided

1 lb. sirloin steak, chopped into very small squares

1 tsp. of ají panca paste

1 medium onion, peeled and chopped

2 garlic cloves, peeled and chopped

1 tsp. ground cumin

1 tsp. ground paprika

1 tomato, chopped

½ tsp. ground black pepper

1 hard-boiled egg, peeled and diced in 8 pieces

½ cup olives

½ cup raisins

1 fresh egg

½ cup ice water

DIRECTIONS

STEP ONE

Combine the flour and 1 teaspoon of salt in a bowl. Add butter. Then work the butter into the flour until it looks like oatmeal.

STEP TWO

Add about ½ cup of ice water, a tablespoon at a time, kneading the mixture lightly until it no longer sticks to your hands.

STEP THREE

Wrap the dough in plastic wrap or put in a plastic bag in the refrigerator for 20 minutes.

STEP FOUR

Heat half the oil in a skillet over medium heat; add the beef and cook, stirring often, for 15 minutes. Transfer to a bowl.

STEP FiVE

In the same pan, heat the remaining oil over medium heat, add the ají panca paste, onion, garlic, cumin, paprika, and then the tomato. Sauté until the onion is very soft, for about 8 minutes.

STEP SiX

Put the beef back in the pan and add remaining salt and pepper. Then turn off the heat and cool completely.

STEP SEVEN

Preheat the oven to 350°F. Take a portion of the dough and use a rolling pin to roll it onto a lightly floured table till it's about ¼ inch thick.

STEP EiGHT

With a large cookie cutter, cut 4-inch circles. Then spoon 1 tablespoon of the filling into the center of each circle. Next add one slice of the hard-boiled egg, one olive, and 2 raisins.

STEP NiNE

Now close the empanadas. Seal the borders by pressing with a fork. Place on an ungreased baking sheet.

whoa!

STEP TEN

In a small bowl, lightly beat the egg with a little water, and brush the empanadas with this mixture. Bake for 20 minutes or until golden.

¡BUEN PROVECHO!